SWEET SIXTEEN

Princess

THE PRINCESS DIARIES, VOLUME VII:
Party Princess

Sweet Sixteen Princess:
A PRINCESS DIARIES BOOK (VOLUME VII AND A HALF)

Illustrated by Chesley McLaren

Princess Lessons:
A PRINCESS DIARIES BOOK

Perfect Princess:
A PRINCESS DIARIES BOOK

Holiday Princess:
A PRINCESS DIARIES BOOK

MEG CABOT

SWEET SIXTEEN
Princess

A PRINCESS DIARIES BOOK

HARPERCOLLINS*PUBLISHERS*

www.harperteen.com

Library of Congress Catalog Card Number: 2006000412

ISBN-10: 0-06-084716-6

ISBN-13: 978-0-06-084716-6

1 2 3 4 5 6 7 8 9 10

❖

First Edition

ACKNOWLEDGMENTS

Many thanks to Beth Ader, Jennifer Brown,
Barb Cabot, Laura Langlie, Abigail McAden,
and especially Benjamin Egnatz.

She could not be made rude and malicious by
the rudeness and malice of those about her.
"A princess must be polite," she said to herself.

A LITTLE PRINCESS
Frances Hodgson Burnett

"So Lana's dad rented the sultan of Brunei's ten-million-dollar yacht for the night, and had Lana and her friends driven out into international waters so they could drink without getting in trouble."

This is what Lilly just called to tell me.

"Lilly," I whispered. "You know you aren't supposed to call me on my cell phone. It is for emergency use only."

"You don't think this is an emergency? Mia, Lana's dad renting the sultan of Brunei's yacht like that? That is a throwdown. He is basically telling your grandmother to bring it."

"I don't have the slightest idea what you're talking about." Because I don't. "And I have to go. I'm at a PTA meeting, for crying out loud."

"Oh, God." I can hear the soundtrack for *Altar Boyz* in the background. Ever since Lilly started going out with J. P. Reynolds-Abernathy the Fourth, she has gotten way into soundtracks from musicals, because J. P.'s dad is a theater producer, and J. P. can get free tickets to any Broadway show he wants, and all of the off-Broadway ones, too. And even the off-off-Broadway ones. "I forgot you had to go to that stupid thing. Sorry I'm not there with you. But . . . well, you know."

I did know. Lilly was serving the last week of a grounding her parents instituted after she was brought home by the NYPD for attacking Andy Milonakis— this kid from downtown whose cable access television show was picked up by MTV—with a Dojo's side salad. Lilly believes Andy's getting a basic cable deal instead of her is a travesty of justice, because her own local show, *Lilly Tells It Like It Is*, is so much better (in her opinion), as it isn't simply entertaining, but also highlights facts she feels her viewers ought to be aware of. Such as the fact that the U.S.'s decision to withhold $34 million from the United Nations Population Fund will lead to two million unwanted pregnancies, 800,000 induced abortions, 4,700 maternal deaths, and 77,000 infant and child deaths worldwide.

Whereas a typical episode of Andy's show features him holding a jar of peanut butter in one hand, a jar of salsa in the other, then making the jars dance with each other.

Lilly is also peeved that Andy is deceiving the American public by allowing them to think he is just a kid, when we both saw him coming out of d.b.a., which is a bar in the East Village that cards. So how did he get in there if he isn't at least twenty-one?

This is what she asked him when she saw him eating a falafel at Dojo's Health Restaurant on St. Marks Place, and why she claims she was forced to hurl her side salad at him, drenching him in tahini dressing, and causing him to call the cops on her.

Thankfully the Drs. Moscovitz talked Andy's legal team out of pressing charges, explaining that Lilly has been experiencing some anger issues since their recent separation.

But that didn't stop them from grounding her.

"So how's the meeting going?" Lilly asked. "Have they gotten to the you-know-what part yet?"

"I wouldn't know, because I'm too distracted,

talking to YOU," I whispered. I had to whisper, because I was sitting in a folding chair in the middle of a row of very uptight-looking parents. Being New Yorkers, they were all, of course, very well dressed, with Prada accessories. But being New Yorkers, they were also all angry about the fact that someone was using a cell phone while someone else—namely, Principal Gupta—was up at the podium, speaking. Also, of course, that Principal Gupta was basically saying she couldn't guarantee that their kids would get into Yale or Harvard, which was making them madder than anything. At $25,000 a year—which is how much tuition at AEHS costs—New York parents expect some return for their investment.

"Well, I'll let you go now, so you can get back to work," Lilly said. "But just FYI: Lana's dad had her flown in to the yacht on the sultan's helicopter, so she could make a spectacular entrance."

"I hope one of the blades cut her head off as she was getting out of it because she forgot to duck," I whispered, avoiding the glare of the lady in front of me, who had turned in her seat to give me a dirty look for talking while Principal Gupta was giving everyone some very important information about the percentage of AEHS graduates who get into Ivy League colleges.

"Well," Lilly said. "No, that didn't happen. But I heard her Azzedine Alaïa skirt flew up over her head and everyone saw that she was wearing a thong."

"Good-bye, Lilly," I said.

"I'm just telling you. Turning sixteen is a big deal. You only do it once. Don't blow it by having one of your stupid loft parties with the Cheetos and Mr. G as a DJ."

"Good-bye, Lilly."

I hung up just as the lady in the seat in front of me turned around to hiss, *Would you please put away that—*"

But she never got to finish, because Lars, who was sitting next to me, casually opened his suit jacket, revealing his sidearm. He was only reaching for a Listerine PocketPak, but the sight of his Glock 9 caused the lady's eyes to widen. She closed her mouth and turned back around in her seat very quickly.

Having an armed bodyguard follow you around everywhere you go can be a total pain in the butt, particularly when it comes to finding private time with your boyfriend.

But there are moments, like that one, when it can actually rock.

Then Principal Gupta asked if there was any outstanding business, and I threw my arm into the air.

Principal Gupta saw me raise my hand. I know she did.

But she totally ignored me, and called on some freshman's mother who wanted to know why the school wasn't doing more to prepare students for the SATs.

She went on to ignore me until she'd answered everyone else's questions. I can't really say that this shows the kind of commitment to youth-oriented issues I'd like to see in my educators, but who am I to complain? Just the president of the student council, is all.

Which is why, after Principal Gupta finally called on me, I saw a lot of parents gathering their Gucci briefcases and Zabar's shopping bags and getting ready to leave. Because who wants to listen to the president of the student council?

"Um, hi," I said, uncomfortably aware of the number of gazes—even if they were only half listening—on me. I may be a princess, and all, but I'm still not used to the whole public-speaking thing, despite Grandmère's best efforts. "I've been asked by a number of AEHS students to address the Parent Teacher Association on the issue of our current physical education curriculum, specifically its emphasis on competitive sports. We feel that spending six weeks learning the finer points of volleyball is a waste of our time and our parents' money. We would prefer our physical education funds be spent on physical education that is just that: education about our physical well-being. We'd like the gymnasium to be converted to an actual fitness center, with weight-training equipment and stationary bikes for spin classes, as well as space for Pilates and t'ai chi.

And for our physical education instructor to act as both a personal trainer and health specialist, who will work with each student individually to create a personal workout and health program targeted to their specific health needs, whether they be weight loss, increase in muscle tone, stress reduction, or simply improved overall health. As you can see"—I pulled out a pile of paper I'd been keeping in my backpack, and began passing the sheets around—"we've assessed the overall costs involved in implementing this kind of health program, and found that it is much more cost-efficient than our current physical education curriculum, if you take into account the staggering amount of money you'll be paying to your child's physicians for treatment of juvenile onset diabetes, asthma, high blood pressure, and the many other dangerous health conditions caused by obesity."

This information was not met with the kind of enthusiastic response we—meaning my fellow student council members, Lilly, Tina, Ling Su, and I— had been hoping for. Parents, I noted, tended to look heavenward, and Principal Gupta glanced at her watch.

"Thank you for this, Mia," she said, holding up the copy of the cost breakdown I'd given her. "But I'm afraid what you're proposing would be far too cost-prohibitive for us at this time—"

"But as you can see by our projections," I said desperately, "if you were to just take a small amount of money away from, say, the Intramural Athletics Fund—"

At *this*, suddenly everyone was paying attention.

"Not the lacrosse team!" one father in a Burberry raincoat bellowed.

"Not soccer," cried another, looking up from his BlackBerry with a panicked expression on his face.

"Not cheerleading!" Mr. Taylor, Shameeka's dad, gave me a dirty look that could have rivaled one of Grandmère's.

"You see the problem, Mia?" Principal Gupta shook her head.

"But if each team just gave up a little—"

"I'm sorry, Mia," Principal Gupta said. "I'm sure

you worked very hard on this. But your track record where financial matters are concerned hasn't exactly been the most stellar—" I couldn't believe she'd be so heartless as to bring up the slight miscalculation that had caused me to bankrupt the student government several weeks earlier. Especially considering the fact that, with the help of my grandmother and her tireless work on behalf of the Genovian olive growers, I had more than replenished the empty coffers. "And I haven't heard any other complaints about our current P.E. curriculum. I move that we conclude this meeting—"

"I second the motion," cried Mrs. Hill, my Gifted and Talented teacher, in an obvious ploy to get home in time for *Dancing with the Stars*.

"This meeting of the Albert Einstein High School Parent Teacher Association is adjourned," Principal Gupta said.

Then she and everybody else booked out of there like winged monkeys were on their tails.

I looked down at Lars, the only person left in the room besides me.

"'The first resistance to social change is to say it's not necessary,'" he said, obviously quoting somebody.

"Sun Tzu?" I asked, since *The Art of War* is Lars's favorite book.

"Gloria Steinem," he confessed. "I was reading one of your mother's magazines in the bathroom the other day." Lars has apparently never heard of the phrase Too Much Information. "Let's go home, Princess."

And so we did.

Wednesday, April 28, 10 p.m.,
limo ride home

How am I ever going to rule an entire country some-day when I can't even get my high school to install a row of stationary bikes in the gym?

At least I have the comforting words of my boyfriend to soothe my frazzled nerves when I get home after a long day of fighting for the rights of the unathletically inclined students of Albert Einstein High. Even if I hardly ever get to talk to him—except via Instant Messaging—because he's so busy with his college courses, and I'm so busy with Geometry, princess lessons, student council, and keeping my baby brother from sticking his tongue in a light socket.

SKINNERBX: Do you realize it's only three days till the big day?

FTLOUIE: What day would that be?

SKINNERBX: Your sweet sixteen!

FTLOUIE: Oh, right. I forgot. Sorry. Stupid school stuff is bumming me out.

SKINNERBX: Poor baby. So what do you want for your birthday?

FTLOUIE: Just you.

SKINNERBX: Are you serious???? Because that can totally be arranged. Doo Pak is going to be gone for the weekend on a Korean Student Association camp-out in the Catskills. . . .

Yikes! All I meant was that I wanted a little time alone with him—something that seems to happen more and more rarely, now that he's opted for accelerated graduation, doing all of his course work in three years instead of four, and his parents splitting up, and all, so that he has to have dinner every Friday night with either his mom or dad, so that each of them feels like they're getting their fair share of Michael time.

And, being the supportive girlfriend that I am, I totally understand about his being there for his parents during this stressful time in their lives. Mr. Dr.

Moscovitz doesn't seem to really like his new rental apartment on the Upper West Side very much, even though he lives just a *New York Times*–throw from Michael's dorm, and can drop by to visit him there anytime he wants (and frequently does so—thank God he has to buzz Michael's room to be let up and can't just come strolling in, or there might have been some awkward moments), and there are plenty of other psychotherapists in the neighborhood for him to hang out with.

And Lilly says life with her mother is practically unbearable, since Mrs. Dr. Moscovitz has put them both on low-carb diets, and banished bagels from the breakfast table entirely, and meets with her trainer, like, four times a week.

But what about MY share of Michael time? I mean, *I* am the girlfriend. Even if I am still not prepared to go as far as he might want to go, making-out-wise.

Which is actually a good thing, considering what Mr. Dr. Moscovitz could have walked in on, that one time.

FTLOUIE: I didn't mean that literally! I meant maybe we could have a nice dinner, just you and me.

SKINNERBX: Oh. Sure. But you can have that anytime. I mean, what do you REALLY want?

What DO I really want? World peace, of course. An end to emissions of the greenhouse gases that are causing global warming. For the Drs. Moscovitz to get back together, so I can see my boyfriend on Friday nights again. To not be a princess anymore. To have things go back to the way they used to be, when things were simpler . . . like that time we all went ice-skating at Rockefeller Center, and I bit my tongue—only without the tongue-biting part.

And the part where Michael was there with Judith Gershner and I was there with Kenny Showalter.

But you know. Aside from that.

But none of these things is something Michael can actually get me. He has no control over world peace, global warming, his parents, or the fact that they close the skating rink at Rockefeller Center on

April 1, so I've never been able to go ice-skating on my birthday.

And he certainly has no control over the fact that I'm a princess. Unfortunately.

FtLouie: Seriously, Michael. Except for a nice dinner, I don't want anything.

SkinnerBx: Are you SURE? Because that's not what you said at Christmas.

What did I say I wanted at Christmas? I can't even remember now. I hope he's not thinking of getting me another Fiesta Giles action figure. Because now that *Buffy*'s only on in reruns, it just makes me sad to look at her and her friends, on their little plastic stands in the cemetery on my dresser. In fact, I've been thinking of replacing them with a lavender plant since the smell of lavender is supposed to be soothing, and I need all the soothing I can get.

Or the *Napoleon Dynamite*–Style Time Machine

Modulus Mr. Gianini confiscated off a kid in his freshman Algebra class and gave to me. Whichever fits better.

Besides, Michael doesn't have time to be bidding on eBay. He needs to spend what little free time he has with me.

Okay, I have to put a kibosh on the gift thing. It's got to be really hard on Michael, figuring out what to get for a girl who can basically get anything she wants from her palace. He's just a poor, hardworking student. It's just not fair to him. Or any boy who might happen to be dating a princess.

FTLOUIE: I have an idea. Let's make a rule: From now on, we can only give each other presents we've MADE.

SKINNERBX: Are you serious?

FTLOUIE: Serious as L. Ron Hubbard was that we're all descended from aliens.

SKINNERBX: Okay. You're on.

WOMYNRULE: POG, are you online with my brother again?

Crud. It's Lilly.

FTLOUIE: Yes. What do you want?

WOMYNRULE: Just to remind you that SHE FLEW IN ON A HELICOPTER.

FTLOUIE: I have flown into tons of things in a helicopter.

Although this is not strictly true. I have only been on a helicopter once, when there was an accident on the FDR and there was no other way to get to the private jet parked at Teterboro.

But I know what Lilly is getting at, and I'm trying to nip it in the bud.

ILUVROMANCE: Mia, you HAVE to have a party. You HAVE to. I know you're upset about what happened at your birthday party last year.

Oh, great! Now Tina's getting in on it, too?

FTLOUIE: Gang up on me, why don't you, everybody.

ILUVROMANCE: Lilly PROMISES what happened last year at your party won't happen this year. We won't play Seven Minutes in Heaven. We are way more mature than that now.

WOMYNRULE: And besides, I'm with J. P. now.

FTLOUIE: You were with Boris then. But it still happened.

WOMYNRULE: But things with Boris were so boring. I mean, where could it go?

ILUVROMANCE: Um. Ahem.

WomynRule: Sorry. I'm sure things with you and Boris are totally different.

ILuvRomance: Dang straight.

WomynRule: But you know what I mean. Things with J. P. are still so . . . well . . . you know.

Did we ever. Because Lilly can talk of hardly anything else. I had never seen her so besotted for a guy. I suppose because J. P. keeps her guessing as to what his real feelings for her are. It seems like all I ever hear from her these days—when she isn't going on about her hatred for Andy Milonakis—is *Do you think he likes me? I mean, we go out, and stuff, and we kiss, but he doesn't say stuff, you know, about how he feels about me. Do you think that's weird? I mean, what kind of guy doesn't talk about his feelings? Well, okay, I know MOST guys don't talk about their feelings. But I mean, what guy who goes to AEHS doesn't want to talk about his feelings? Who isn't gay, I mean?*

As if *I'm* supposed to know.

ILUVROMANCE: Has he still not said the L word, Lilly?

WOMYNRULE: He hasn't even said the G word. As in, that I'm his girlfriend.

FTLOUIE: Have YOU said the L word to HIM? Or the B word?

WOMYNRULE: Of COURSE not. We've only been going out for a little over a month. I don't want to scare him off.

FTLOUIE: Faint heart never won fair lady.

WOMYNRULE: Stop quoting Gilbert and Sullivan at me. I want him to say the L word first. Is that such a crime? WHY WON'T HE SAY IT????

ILUVROMANCE: Well, you know J. P. has always been something of a loner. He probably just doesn't know how to act around girls.

WomynRule: Do you really think so?

FtLouie: Totally. Oh my God, you guys, check it out: J. P.'s like the Beast from *Beauty and the Beast*, you know, when Belle first comes to live in the palace, and the Beast is all mean to her? Because, just like the Beast was alone in his castle for all those years, J. P. sat by himself at a lunch table for a really long time, so maybe he isn't entirely sure how people are supposed to interact, because he hasn't had all that much experience with human interaction—JUST LIKE THE BEAST!!! So he may come off as gruff or nonemotional, when I'm sure the opposite is true—JUST LIKE THE BEAST!!!!

WomynRule: Mia, I know *Beauty and the Beast* is your favorite musical, and all. But I think that's sort of stretching it.

ILuvRomance: No, I think Mia is right. All J. P. needs is the right woman to unlock his heart—which up until now he has kept in a cold, hard shell for his own emotional protection—and he will be like an unstoppable volcano of passion.

WOMYNRULE: In that case, why hasn't he exploded already? Unless you're implying I'm not the right woman to unlock his heart.

ILUVROMANCE: I'm not saying that! I'm just saying that it won't be easy.

FTLOUIE: Yeah. Like it wasn't easy for Belle to win the Beast's trust.

WOMYNRULE: Whatever! It took her, like, two songs!

ILUVROMANCE: Yeah, but real life isn't like a musical. Unfortunately.

FTLOUIE: Maybe if you said you loved him first, it would cause the first crack in his hard outer shell. . . .

WOMYNRULE: I AM NOT SAYING I LOVE HIM FIRST!!!!

SKINNERBX: Mia? Are you still there?

My boyfriend! I had gotten so involved talking about Lilly's boyfriend, I totally forgot about my own!

FTLOUIE: Of course I am. Hang on a minute.

FTLOUIE: You guys, I have to go, but one last thing: I AM NOT HAVING A SWEET SIXTEEN PARTY AND THAT'S FINAL. GOT IT?

WOMYNRULE: God, alright already. You don't have to shout.

ILUVROMANCE: Mia, no one wants you to do anything you don't want to do. But your sweet sixteen IS a big deal. . . .

FTLOUIE: NO PARTY.

WOMYNRULE: Well, better make sure your grandma knows that, then.

FTLOUIE: Wait. What is THAT supposed to mean?

WOMYNRULE: Nothing. I have to go now.

FTLOUIE: LILLY!!! ARE YOU AND GRANDMÈRE PLOTTING SOMETHING BEHIND MY BACK AGAIN????

WOMYNRULE: terminated

FTLOUIE: I'm going to kill her.

ILUVROMANCE: She can't help it. You know how upset she's been since her parents' separation. Not to mention this Andy Milonakis thing. And the fact that J. P. won't admit his true feelings for her. Oops, I hear my mom calling. I have to go. Bye!

ILUVROMANCE: terminated

Great. Just great.

FTLOUIE: Michael, do you know if your sister and my grandmother are planning something for my birthday? Like a surprise party?

SKINNERBX: Not that I'm aware of. Can you imagine what kind of party those two would come up with?

Actually, I can:
The kind of party I'd really, really hate.

Thursday, April 29, Homeroom

I asked my mom at breakfast this morning if Grandmère and Lilly were planning a surprise party for my sweet sixteen, and she choked on her fresh-squeezed OJ from Papaya King and went, "Sweet Jesus, I hope not."

To which Mr. Gianini added, "Don't expect me to chaperone if they are. I saw enough grinding at the Nondenominational Winter Dance this year to last me a lifetime."

Which is true. Grinding does seem to be all the rage around Albert Einstein High lately. I wish it were krumping, instead. But no. My peers (all except for Michael, who is opposed to grinding for reasons he has yet to share with me, beyond saying it's "stupid looking") seem only to want to rub their private parts against one another.

Too bad they won't let us do THAT in PE.

"I thought you didn't want a party this year," my mom said. "Because of what happened at your party last year."

"I don't," I said. "But, you know . . . people don't always listen to me."

By people, of course, I meant Grandmère. As my mom well knew.

"Well, you can rest easy," my mom said. "I haven't heard anything about Lilly and your grandmother planning any party."

I quizzed Lilly at length about my suspicions in the limo on the way to school, but she never once cracked.

Perhaps I was only imagining the whole Grandmère/Lilly plot to fete me against my will.

Which isn't any wonder, really, if you think about all the stuff they've gotten up to behind my back in the past. Really, they are like the Snape/Malfoy pairing of the Muggle world. Only without the capes.

Thursday, April 29, Gifted and Talented

I observed J. P. closely all through lunch to see if I could detect any signs that he might explode in a volcano of passion, as Tina suggested he was going to someday.

He must have noticed me staring at him though, because at one point when Lilly got up to get a second helping of mac and cheese (her mother's low-carb diet has had the opposite effect she'd evidently hoped for where Lilly is concerned—it has only turned Lilly into even more of a raging carboholic), he looked at me and went, "Mia. Do I have something on my face?"

I was like, "No. Why?"

"Because you keep looking at me."

Busted! How embarrassing!

"Sorry," I muttered into my Diet Coke, hoping he wouldn't notice how I was blushing. Only how could he not, under the unforgiving glare of the fluorescent overheads? (Note to self: Look into cost of getting new, more flattering lighting in caf.) "I was just . . . checking something."

"Checking what?"

"Nothing," I said hastily, and dug into my bean salad.

"Mia," J. P. started to say, in a soft—but deep—voice, that (not surprisingly, considering the fact that Boris, across the table, had his violin out, and was showing Tina, Ling Su, and Perin how easy it was to pluck out the chords to the Foo Fighters' "Best of You") only I could hear. "Do you—"

But he never got to finish whatever it was he was going to say to me, because at that moment Lilly returned.

"Can you believe they were out of mac and cheese?" she asked. "I had to settle for four slices of bread and a bag of Doritos." She seemed to overcome her disappointment pretty quickly, though, if how fast she chowed down those Doritos is any indication.

I wonder what J. P. was going to say to me?

I think Tina is definitely right. One of these days, he's going to blow like Mount Vesuvius. There will be no controlling J. P.'s eruption of passion when it finally happens.

I walked into Grandmère's suite at the Plaza only to
be attacked by this woman with purple hair in a pair
of lowriders who went, "Oh, great, she's here," and
tried to stick a portable microphone pack down the
back of my shirt.

"What are you DOING?" I demanded.

Fortunately Lars was with me, and he stepped in
front of the woman and said, looking down at her all
menacingly, "May I help you?"

Ms. Purple Hair had to crane her neck to see
Lars's face. Apparently she didn't like what she
saw up there, since she took a few stumbling steps
backward and went, "Um . . . Lewis? We've got a
slight . . . or, I guess I should say, big—*really* big—
problem."

Which is when this skinny guy in a pair of fancy
red eyeglasses came hurrying out of Grandmère's
living room, going, "Oh, great, she's here. Princess
Mia, I'm so glad to meet you. I'm Lewis, and this is

my assistant, Janine—" He indicated the purple-haired woman, who was still staring up at Lars like she was looking at King Kong, or someone, and seemed unable to utter a sound. "If you'd just let Janine put your mic on, we can go ahead and get started."

I didn't bother asking Lewis what it was we could go ahead and get started. Instead, I went, "Excuse me," and walked past him, and right up to Grandmère, who was sitting in her pink Louis XV chair with her hair all freshly set, her makeup perfect, and a trembling, nearly hairless toy poodle in her lap.

"Oh, Amelia, good, you're here," she said. "Where's your mic?"

"Grandmère," I said, noticing for the first time the cameraman hovering by her shoulder. "What is going on? Who are these people? Why is that man filming us?"

"He isn't going to be able to use any of the footage, Mia, if you don't put a mic on," Grandmère said irritably. "Janine! Janine, would you please put a mic on her?"

Lewis came in, bobbing his spiky-haired head.

"Um, yes, Your Highness, well, Janine tried, see, but there appears to be a problem—"

"What problem?" Grandmère demanded imperiously.

"She, um," Lewis said, looking scared. But not of Lars. Of Grandmère. "Wouldn't let Janine put it on her."

Grandmère swung the evil eye she'd been focusing on Lewis onto me.

"Amelia," she said coldly. "Kindly allow the violet-haired young lady to put a microphone on you, so that we can get this out of the way. I have a dinner engagement I don't care to miss."

"Nobody's putting anything on me," I said, so loudly that Rommel, in Grandmère's lap, put his ears back and whimpered, "until someone explains to me what's going on."

"Oh, sorry," Lewis said, looking mortified. "I thought you knew. I had no idea. Janine and I—oh, and that's Rafe, with the camera"—Rafe, a burly guy in a bandanna, waved at me from behind his camera lens—"are from MTV, and you're currently being filmed for a very special episode of MTV's hit reality series, *My Super Sweet Sixteen.*"

I looked from Lewis to Grandmère to Rafe—I couldn't see Janine, because she was still out in the foyer with Lars—and back again.

"What?" I said.

"*My Super Sweet Sixteen* is a reality television series on MTV," Lewis explained, as if that were the part I was having trouble with. "Each week it features a different teen getting ready to celebrate his or her sixteenth birthday party. We film all the preparations leading up to the party, and then the party itself. It's one of our most popular shows. Surely you've seen it."

"Oh, I've seen it, all right," I said. "Which is why I'm out of here. Bye."

And I started to leave.

BECAUSE I KNEW IT!!!! I KNEW MY GRANDMOTHER HAD BEEN UP TO SOMETHING!!!!!

But I didn't get very far, on account of tripping over a power cord for one of the lights they'd set up.

Also on account of Grandmère standing up (dislodging a very surprised Rommel, who fortunately, due to years of practice, was able to land on his feet) and saying, "Amelia! Sit down this instant!"

It's her voice. There's just something about that voice that MAKES you do what she says. I don't know how she does it, but she does.

I found myself sinking down onto the couch, nursing the shin I'd bonked against her coffee table.

"That's better," Grandmère said in a totally different tone. She sank back down into her fancy pink chair. "Now, let's try that again. Amelia, these nice people are going to televise your sweet sixteen birthday party on a special edition of their reality series. This will generate a great deal of publicity for the country of Genovia, over which you will one day rule, and which is currently suffering from an almost total lack of American tourists, thanks to the weak dollar and your father's recent decision to limit the number of cruise ships that may dock there to twelve per week. Now, please allow Janine to put a microphone on you so that we can begin. I don't want to keep my dinner date waiting. Mr. Castro is a very impatient man."

I took a deep breath. Then I went—even though I really, really didn't want to know—"What sweet sixteen birthday party?"

"The one I am throwing for you," Grandmère said. "I shall be flying you and one hundred of your closest friends in the royal jet to Genovia, where you'll be met at the airport by horse-drawn carriages and taken immediately to the palace for a champagne brunch, followed by an all-expenses-paid shopping trip to boutiques such as Chanel and Louis Vuitton on the Rue de Prince Phillipe for the girls, and a trip to the Genovian beach for private jet ski lessons for the boys. Then it's back to the palace for massages and fashion and beauty makeovers. Then everyone is invited to a black-tie ball in your honor, at which Destiny's Child, who have agreed to reunite for one night only on your behalf, will perform their greatest hits. After which I will have everyone flown home the following morning so that they arrive back in America in time for school on Monday."

I could only stare at her. I knew my mouth was open. I also knew that Rafe was filming the whole thing.

But I couldn't close my mouth. And I couldn't summon the words to ask Rafe to put his camera down.

Because I was totally FREAKED!!!!

Champagne brunches? All-expenses-paid shopping trips to Louis Vuitton? Massages? Destiny's Child? One hundred of my closest friends?

I don't even KNOW one hundred people, much less have that many friends.

"It's going to be spectacular," Lewis said, pulling up a chair so he could peer at me more closely through the lenses of his red-framed glasses—which kind of resembled plastic scissor handles, I noticed. "It'll be the most fantastic episode of *My Super Sweet Sixteen* ever. We're even changing the name of the series just for your episode . . . we're calling it *My Super ROYAL Sweet Sixteen*. Your party, Princess, is going to make every other party ever featured on this show look like a five-year-old's birthday party at Chuck E. Cheese."

"And," Grandmère said—up close, I could see that she had really layered on the pancake makeup for the benefit of the camera—"it will attract millions of eager tourists to Genovia, once they've seen all that our little country has to offer by way of exclusive, high-end shopping, world-class entertainment, seaside recreation opportunities, fine dining, luxury accommodations, and old-world hospitality."

I looked from Grandmère to Lewis and then back again, my mouth still open.

Then I jumped up and ran for the door.

Thursday, April 29, the loft

Well, who wouldn't have run? This has got to be, hands down, the most disturbing thing she's ever done. Seriously. I mean, MTV? *My Super ROYAL Sweet Sixteen*? Has she lost her mind?

She called Mom to complain, of course. About me. She says I'm being selfish and ungrateful. She says all I ever think about is myself, and that this is a tremendous opportunity for Genovia to finally get some good press after all the negative news stories about it lately, considering the snail thing and almost getting thrown out of the EU, and all. She says if I really cared about the country over which I will someday rule, I would accept her generous gift and agree to be filmed doing so.

And I DO really care about Genovia. I DO.

BUT I DO NOT WANT A SWEET SIX-TEEN BIRTHDAY PARTY!!!!!

And I particularly do not want one that is going to be BROADCAST AROUND THE COUNTRY ON MTV!!!!!!!

Why is that so hard for people to understand?????

At least Mom's on my side. When she heard what Grandmère (and MTV) had planned, her lips got all small, the way they do when she's really, really mad. Then she said, "Don't worry, honey. I'll take care of it."

Then she went to make some phone calls.

To my dad in Genovia, I hope. Or possibly an insane asylum, so that Grandmère can be locked up at last for her own—and my—protection.

But I suppose that's a little too much to ask.

Why can't I have a NORMAL grandma? One who'd make me a cake for my birthday, instead of hosting a transcontinental royal slumber party for me, and allow a cable network to FILM it?

WHY?

Friday, April 30, lunch

I was regaling everyone at lunch about Grandmère's crazy scheme—I had purposefully not told anyone about it, including Lilly, just so I could tell everyone about it at the same time, because ever since J. P. started sitting with us at lunch, there's sort of been this contest between us girls to see who can make him laugh the hardest, because, well, J. P. seems like he could use a laugh, being a bottled-up volcano of passion, and all.

Not that anyone has really ADMITTED that's what we do. Try to see who can make J. P. laugh the hardest, that is.

But we totally do.

At least, I do.

Anyway, I was telling everyone about Lewis-with-the-scissor-handle glasses, and Janine-of-the-purple-hair, and they were laughing—especially J. P., particularly when I got to the part about the sex-segregated shopping for girls and jet-skiing for boys—when Lilly put down her chicken parm on a roll and was like, "Frankly, Mia, I think it was extremely uncool of you to turn down your grandmother's generous offer to throw you such a fantastic party."

I just stared at her with my mouth open, the way I'd stared at Grandmère and Lewis the night before.

"I do think it would be kind of neat to fly to Genovia for the weekend," Perin said softly, from the other side of the table.

"I could totally use a Louis Vuitton violin case," Boris said.

"But only the girls would be allowed to shop," I pointed out to him. "You'd have to be jet-skiing with the boys. And you know how you get that allergic reaction to sand-flea bites."

"Yeah," Boris grumbled. "But Tina could have bought one for me."

"You guys," I said. I couldn't believe what I was hearing. "*Hello.* Have you ever even seen that show, *My Super Sweet Sixteen*? They totally try to make the people on it look bad! On purpose. That's the POINT of the series."

"Not necessarily," Lilly said. "I think the point

of the series is to show how some American young people choose to celebrate their coming-of-age—which in this country is at sixteen—and to convey to audiences what a difficult and yet joyous time it can be, as sweet sixteens struggle on the threshold of adulthood, not quite a child anymore, not yet a man or woman. . . ."

Everyone stared at her. J. P. was the one who finally said, "Um, I always thought the point of the series was to show stupid people spending way too much money on something that ultimately has no meaning."

"TOTALLY!" I burst out. I couldn't believe J. P. had put it so exactly right. Well, I could, of course, because J. P. is a wordsmith, like me, and aspires to a literary career of some sort, just like I do.

But I also couldn't because, well, he's a guy, and most of the time, guys just don't GET stuff like that.

"Lilly," I said, "don't you remember that episode where those girls invited five hundred of their closest friends to that rock concert they gave for themselves at that night club, and they made that big deal out of not letting freshmen come, and had the ones who crashed thrown out by bouncers? Oh, and charged their friends admission to get in? To their own birthday party?"

"And then gave the money to charity," Lilly pointed out.

"But still!" I said. "What about that girl who had herself carried into her party on a bed held on the shoulders of eight guys from the local crew team, then forced all her friends to watch a fashion show with herself as the only model?"

"No one is saying you have to do any of those things, Mia," Lilly glowered.

"Lilly, that's not the point. Think about it," I said. "I'm the princess of Genovia. I'm supposed to be a role model. I support causes like Greenpeace and Housing for the Hopeful. What kind of role model would I be if I showed up on TV, spent all that money flying my friends to Genovia and had a huge shopping spree and rock concert, just for them?"

"The kind who really appreciates her friends," Lilly said, "and wants to do something nice for them."

"I do really appreciate you guys," I said, a little bit hurt by this. "And I definitely think each and every one of you deserves a trip to Genovia for shopping sprees and free concerts. But think about it. How would it look, spending all that money on a *birthday party*?"

"It's going to look like your grandmother really, really loves you," Lilly said.

"No, it's not. It's going to look like I'm the biggest selfish spoiled brat on the planet. And if my grandmother really, really loved me," I said, "she'd spend all that money on something I really wanted—like helping to feed AIDS orphans in Ethiopia, or even . . . I don't know. Getting stationary bikes for spinning classes at AEHS!—not something I don't care about at all."

"Mia's right," Tina said. "Although . . . I've always wanted to see Destiny's Child in concert."

"And I've always wanted to see the art collection at the Genovian palace," said Ling Su, a little wistfully.

"I could totally use a makeover," Perin said.

"Maybe then people would stop thinking I'm a boy."

"You guys!" I was shocked. "You can't be serious! You'd want to let yourselves be filmed doing all that stuff? And have it be shown on MTV?"

Tina, Ling Su, Perin, and Boris looked at one another. Then they looked at me, and shrugged. "Yeah."

"Admit it, Mia," Lilly said angrily. "This doesn't have anything to do with you being afraid of looking selfish on TV. It has to do with you still holding what happened at your party last year against me." Lilly's lips got as small as—maybe even smaller than—my mom's had, the night before. "And so you're going to make everybody here suffer for it."

Silence roared across the lunch table after Lilly dropped this little bombshell. Boris suddenly didn't seem to know where to look, and so settled for staring at the leftover buffalo bites on his tray. Tina turned red and reached for her Diet Coke, sucking very noisily on the straw sticking out of it.

Or maybe her sucking just seemed noisy, compared to how quiet everyone had gotten.

Except of course for J. P., who, out of everyone there, was the only person who had no idea what Lilly had done at my fifteenth birthday party. Even Perin knew, having been filled in about it by Shameeka during a particularly boring French class. In French, no less.

"Wait," J. P. said. "What happened at Mia's party last year?"

"Something," Lilly said fiercely, her eyes very bright behind her contacts, "that's never going to happen again."

"Okay," J. P. said. "But what was it? And why does Mia still hold it against you?"

But Lilly didn't say anything. Instead, she scooted her chair back and ran—pretty melodramatically, if you ask me—to the ladies' room.

I didn't go after her. Neither did Tina. Instead, Ling Su did, saying, with a sigh, "I guess it's my turn, anyway."

The bell rang right after that. As we were picking up our trays to take them back to the jet line, J. P. turned to me and asked, "So are you ever going to tell me what that was all about?"

But, remembering what Tina had said about the volcano of passion, I shook my head. Because I don't want him exploding all over ME.

Friday, April 30,
between lunch and *G&T*

At least Michael is on my side about it. The party thing, I mean. Because when I called him just now on my cell (even though, technically, this was not an emergency) to tell him what Grandmère had planned, he said, "When you say transcontinental slumber party, do you mean that we'd get to sleep in the same room?"

To which I replied, "Most assuredly not."

"And you haven't changed your mind about having sex with me now?" Michael asked. "As opposed to after your senior prom?"

"I think you would have been the first to know if I had," I said, blushing deeply, as I always do when this topic comes up.

"Oh," Michael said. "Well, then I'm on your side."

"But, Michael," I said, just to make sure I understood. Communication between couples is so important, as we all know from Dr. Phil. "Don't you want to go jet-skiing and see Destiny's Child?"

"Jet skis are really harmful to the environment, being far more polluting than other two-stroke motors, not to mention that marine mammal experts have testified that personal watercraft activity near seals, sea lions, and elephant seals disturbs normal rest and social interaction, and causes stampedes into the water that can separate seal pups from adult mothers," Michael said. "And, no offense, but Destiny's Child is a girl band."

"Michael," I said, shocked. "Don't be sexist!"

"I'm not saying they aren't immensely talented, not to mention sexy as hell," Michael said. "But let's face it: Only girls like to listen to them."

"I guess you're right," I admitted.

"But you should let the people who love you throw *some* kind of party for you," Michael said. "Not necessarily on MTV, but you know . . . *something*. Turning sixteen is a big deal. And it's not like you had a bat mitzvah or anything."

"But—"

"I know you're still emotionally scarred by what

my sister did at your last party," Michael said. "But maybe you should give her another chance. After all, she seems totally crazy about J. P. I highly doubt she's going to cheat on him in a closet with a Tibetan busboy."

"I think Jangbu was Nepalese," I said.

"Whatever. The point is, Mia, your sweet sixteen should be a birthday you'll remember for all time. It should be special. Don't let Lilly—or your grandmother—dictate how you celebrate it. But DO celebrate it."

"Thanks, Michael," I said, feeling truly moved by his words. He is so *wise* sometimes.

"And if you change your mind about the sex thing," he joked, "call me."

And other times, so not.

I think I finally get it. What's going on with Lilly and this *My Super Royal Sweet Sixteen* thing, I mean.

I figured it out when Lilly looked up from the issue of *The 'Zine*—the school literary magazine—she is currently working on, and said, in an effort to get me to change my mind about the birthday thing, "It may be the only way some of us are ever going to get on MTV!"

And then it all became clear. Why it is that Lilly is so adamant about my letting Grandmère go ahead with her birthday plan, I mean.

Think about it. Where on earth would GRAND-MÈRE have gotten the idea to go on *My Super Sweet Sixteen*? She's never seen that show. She doesn't even know what MTV *is*. Somebody had to have planted that idea in her head.

And I'm betting that somebody is named Lilly Moscovitz.

I KNEW IT!!!! I KNEW THEY WERE IN

ON SOMETHING TOGETHER!!!!

They really ARE like Snape and Malfoy. Minus the capes.

"Lilly," I said, trying to sound understanding, and not accusatory. Because Dr. Phil says this is the best way to handle conflict resolution. "I'm sorry Andy Milonakis got his own show, and you didn't. And I do think it's a travesty of justice, because your show is way more intelligent AND entertaining than his is. And I'm sorry your parents are separated, and I'm sorry your boyfriend won't say the L word. But I am not violating my most sacred principles just so that you can finally reach your target demographic. I'm sorry, but there's not going to be any Super ROYAL Sweet Sixteen Slumber Party in Genovia. And that's final. And you can tell my grandmother that."

Lilly blinked a few times. "Me? Tell your grandmother? Why would I tell your grandmother anything?"

"Oh, please," I said. "Like you weren't the one

who put the bug in her ear about the show *My Super Sweet Sixteen*."

"Is that what you think?" Lilly demanded, throwing down the pen she was using to mark up *'Zine* submissions. "Well, what if I did? SOMEONE should do something for your birthday, since you're so opposed to anyone so much as *mentioning* it."

"And whose fault is that?" I asked her. "After you ruined my birthday party last year—not to mention what you did at Christmas, in Genovia—"

"I SAID I WAS SORRY FOR THAT!" Lilly shrieked. "WHAT DO I HAVE TO DO TO MAKE YOU FREAKING TRUST ME THAT IT WON'T HAPPEN AGAIN?"

"Prove it," I said, my voice sounding very quiet, compared to hers. Which, considering that she was yelling her head off, was kind of no surprise. Lucky for her Mrs. Hill was in the teacher's lounge, calling Visa to get her credit limit extended.

"And how am I supposed to do that?" Lilly wanted to know.

I thought about it. What COULD Lilly do to prove that she would never again betray my trust by making out with (or playing strip bowling with) relative strangers at some party I, or one of my family members, was hosting?

I thought about making her sing "Don't Cha" ("Don't cha wish your girlfriend was hot like me?") at the next pep rally, in front of the whole school. That would certainly have been entertaining, not to mention interesting, considering how Principal Gupta might react.

But then I thought of something that would be even MORE interesting.

"Tell J. P. that you love him," I said.

I had the satisfaction of seeing all the blood drain from Lilly's face.

"Mia," she breathed. "I can't. You know I can't. We all agreed—boys like to make the first move. They don't like it when girls say the L word first. They run from them . . . like startled fawns."

I felt a little twinge of guilt. Because she was

right. What I was asking her to do might very well cause J. P. to drop her like a hot potato.

But it was like there was some kind of crazy little mean elf inside me, making me say it, anyway.

"Don't you think you're underestimating J. P.?" I asked. "I mean, he is not like a typical boy. Does a typical boy know the score to *Avenue Q* by heart? Who isn't gay, I mean?"

"No," Lilly said hesitantly.

"Does a typical boy write poems about the school administration and his desire to bring it down?"

"Um," Lilly said. "I guess not."

"And does a typical boy pick all the corn out of his chili?"

"Okay," Lilly said. "Granted, J. P. is not a typical boy. But, Mia, what you're asking me to do . . . tell him that I love him . . . it could permanently damage—or end—my relationship with him."

"Or," I said, "it could unloose the lava flow of passion that you and I both know is bubbling just underneath the surface of J. P.'s cool exterior."

Lilly blinked at me. "Have you been reading Tina's romance novels?" she wanted to know.

I ignored that. Or the mean little elf did, really.

"If you really and truly want me to forgive you for all those times you ruined my parties," I said, "you will tell J. P. you love him."

Even as the words were coming out of my mouth, I couldn't believe I was saying them. I don't even know *why* I was saying them. What did I care whether or not Lilly told J. P. she loved him?

Although it would definitely cut down on her whining about his not using the L word. And I *was* kind of interested to see what he'd do in response. You know, in a fun, social-experiment kind of way.

Lilly didn't look like she agreed with me, though. About it being a fun social experiment to tell J. P. she loved him. In fact, she kind of looked like she wanted to barf.

Which prompted me to ask, "You *do* love him, don't you? I mean, you've only been going on about how great he is for the past month and a half."

"Of *course* I love him," Lilly said. "I'm crazy about him. Who wouldn't be? He's, like, the world's most perfect guy—smart, funny, sensitive, hot, tall, not gay, and yet still obsessed with *Wicked*, *Everwood*, and *Gilmore Girls*. . . . That's why I don't want to ruin it—what I have with him!"

Which was when I heard myself say, "It's the only thing I want for my birthday. Besides world peace. Your telling J. P. that you love him, I mean."

What was WRONG with me? That wasn't ME talking. It was the mean little elf inside my mouth, making it move and say things I didn't actually mean.

Maybe this is what happens when you turn sixteen. A mean little elf moves inside your body and starts controlling your words and actions. Funny how they've never mentioned anything about THAT on *My Super Sweet Sixteen*. Or on *Dr. Phil*.

"This is just like when Henry II asked his knights to kill the Archbishop of Canterbury," Lilly said in a small voice.

"Or when Rachel asked Ross to drink the glass of

leftover fat in order to prove his love on *Friends*," I said. Because I wasn't talking about *murdering* J. P., for crying out loud.

But was Lilly going to drink the fat?

That was the question she seemed to be struggling with as she murmured, "I have to go to the office to get something photocopied," and wandered from the G and T room in a sort of daze.

"Mia," Boris—who had just been headed into the supply closet to practice his latest piece when Lilly and I had started fighting, and so of course he'd stopped to watch (though he'd pretended to be listening to his iPod)—said. "What are you *doing*?"

Even though Boris is already sixteen, he apparently hasn't met his mean little elf. Maybe boys don't get them when they turn sixteen.

Still, I can't say I appreciated his tone. I mean, he knows from firsthand experience how difficult Lilly can be to deal with sometimes.

Really, Lilly should be grateful he hasn't said anything to J. P. about the details surrounding their breakup. I don't think even the Beast would have appreciated hearing about how Belle played Seven Minutes in Heaven with a guy who wasn't her boyfriend right in front of said boyfriend.

I'm just saying.

Friday, April 30, the Plaza

I entered Grandmère's suite super carefully, looking around for any cameramen or purple-haired girls who might be lurking in the shadows.

But Grandmère seemed to be the only one in there. Well, Grandmère and Rommel, who I discreetly checked for mics. But he appeared not to have any secret bugs tucked into his purple velour sweat suit. That I could find, anyway.

"Oh, for God's sake, Amelia," Grandmère said, apparently realizing what I was doing. "They're gone. You made your position on the subject perfectly clear yesterday. There isn't going to be any television show. At least, not one featuring you."

"What do you mean?" I asked, throwing down my backpack and making myself comfy on the couch.

Grandmère raised an eyebrow at me. "Amelia," she said. "Feet."

I took my feet off her coffee table. I guess the mean elf inside me is also kind of a slob.

"What do you mean, at least not one featuring me?" I asked.

"Well," Grandmère said. "You didn't want to go. Although you didn't have to have your mother telephone your father, you know, Amelia. You could simply have TOLD me you didn't want to appear on *My Super Royal Sweet Sixteen*."

"I DID," I said.

"In any case," Grandmère said. "It was too late to change all the plans I made for your party, so Lewis has arranged for another young person to take your place."

"Another young person?" I gaped at her. "Like who? A Mia Thermopolis look-alike?"

"Certainly not," Grandmère said with a soft snort. "Instead of your sweet sixteen, we'll be celebrating the sweet sixteen of someone else—a young man named Andy Milonakis."

My jaw dropped. "You're taking ANDY MILONAKIS to GENOVIA?"

"There's no need to shout, Amelia. And yes, I

am. Lewis is very pleased with the way things have turned out. I'll be taking this boy and ten of his friends—I thought one hundred was a bit excessive, considering he's not even a family member—to Genovia, to do all the things you and your friends could have done for YOUR birthday, if you weren't so selfish and stubborn. They're calling it *Andy's Super Royal Sweet Sixteen*. Lewis promises that it's going to reach millions of viewers. The glories of Genovia will soon be known to that hard-to-reach eighteen-to-thirty-nine-year-old male demographic."

For once, the mean little elf in me was silent. It didn't, for instance, goad me into suggesting that the eighteen-to-thirty-nine-year-old males who enjoy Andy Milonakis's show probably still live at home with their parents and can't afford a trip to Genovia.

It didn't prompt me to mention that the ten friends Andy would be bringing with him to Genovia were probably going to include—at least judging from his TV show—his dog, Woobie, the guy who owns the cherry ice stand on the corner, and Rivka, the rooster-headed chicken lady, this old woman Andy forces to wear a hat with two chicken legs sticking out of it.

It also didn't urge me to tell Grandmère that Andy Milonakis probably turned sixteen ten years ago, and was just using her to get publicity for his show, the same way she was using him to get publicity for Genovia.

Instead, I said, meaning it, "Grandmère. This is the best birthday present you've ever given me."

To which Grandmère replied with a slight snort, and a sip of her Sidecar.

But I could tell she was pleased.

Saturday, May 1, 10 a.m., the loft

Well. That's it. I'm sixteen. At last. I can now legally have sex in most European countries, including Genovia, and just about every state in America. Except the one I actually live in.

Oh, yeah, and I can apply for a learner's permit to drive. Which I guess would be a big deal, if I didn't have to go everywhere in a limo, anyway.

Mr. G made real homemade waffles for breakfast, and then he and Mom and Rocky all sat around the table and watched me open my presents from them, which included, from Mom, a vintage Run Katie Run T-shirt; from Mr. G, an iTunes gift certificate for 50 song downloads (yes!); and from Rocky, a big pile of Mead wide-ruled composition notebooks with black marbled covers, for future journal entries and novel-writing attempts.

Even Fat Louie got me something—a Fiesta Giles action figure to replace the one I sold on eBay to get Michael an original 1977 *Star Wars* poster last Christmas.

Oh, well.

Mom apologized on Dad's behalf for his not having called or gotten me anything, but said he hadn't forgotten—he's just been super busy with Parliament.

I said Dad already got me a present—he yelled at Grandmère and got me out of having to be on *My Super Royal Sweet Sixteen*.

That is a gift for the ages.

Then Michael called and asked if I wanted to have the romantic birthday dinner I'd suggested we have in the first place. I said yes, and went to begin beautifying myself. Because even though our dinner isn't for eight hours, it never hurts to get a head start on the beautifying. Especially if you need a lot of beautifying, the way I do.

Saturday, May 1, 5 p.m.

I've received birthday e-mails from around the world! Not just from my friends (although I've heard from all of them, too—well, all except for Lilly, but that's no surprise: She's probably still sulking over her big chance at appearing on MTV being blown), but from other royals such as Prince William and some of my Grimaldi cousins, including the one no one even knew I had, another illegitimate royal just like me, only this one courtesy of Prince Albert of Monaco.

But best of all was the CUTEST e-card from Princess Aiko of Japan, my favorite royal of all time (besides my dad, of course), of a chihuahua wearing a tiara.

Just had a lovely afternoon of made-for-TV-movie viewing . . . which is the best way to spend any birthday, if you ask me. Saw a Kellie Martin double feature, *Her Last Chance*, in which Kellie plays a teen drug addict falsely accused of her boyfriend's murder, and *Her Hidden Truth*, in which Kellie plays a teen delinquent falsely accused of her family's murder.

Good stuff.

Now I seriously have to get ready. Michael will be here to pick me up in one hour. I wonder where we're going to dinner????

I've been had. I can't believe they ALL knew—well, everybody except Grandmère—and none of them said anything. . . .

Oh, well. I guess it's no more than I deserve, being such a party pooper, and all.

Only if I had known in advance about THIS party, I wouldn't have pooped on it. I SWEAR! It's like they all got together and tried to figure out what all my favorite things were, and then—

Well, okay, better start from the beginning:

Michael showed up at six on the dot for our date—even though I'd told him it wasn't necessary to pick me up, since I am perfectly capable of meeting him somewhere, given my limo and personal bodyguard. But he'd insisted. It never occurred to me to wonder why until we stepped outside (with Lars, who kept smirking—but I just assumed that was because he'd gotten Janine-from-MTV's phone number. . . . I'd caught him text messaging her the day before) and got into the limo, and Michael didn't even tell the driver where to go.

But Hans started heading uptown, anyway, like they'd already agreed on their destination.

"Michael," I said, starting to get suspicious. Actually, I'd already been a little suspicious something might be going on when Mom and Mr. G, right before Michael arrived, had announced they were taking Rocky to see the latest Winnie the Pooh movie over at the Loews Cineplex. I mean, the kid is barely one. And they were taking him to the movies? At night?

But I wasn't thinking about that when the limo started heading uptown without Michael saying anything.

"Where are we going?" I asked him.

But he just grinned and took my hand.

It was when the limo hit Midtown that I started getting even more suspicious. Michael can't afford to take me out to eat anywhere in Midtown. Anywhere I'd want to go, anyway.

And then when the limo pulled up alongside Rockefeller Center, I REALLY started freaking out.

Where could we possibly be going in or around Rockefeller Center? The rink was closed on account of it being too warm now for ice-skating.

Except . . .

Except that as we pulled up to it, I saw that it wasn't. Closed, I mean.

Instead, the skating rink was closed *in*—with a giant white tent, like the kind people rent for weddings.

Seriously. The rink at Rockefeller Center was covered in a giant white tent. People were standing all around it, taking pictures and pointing, like the tent had just magically mushroomed there overnight.

You couldn't tell what was going on underneath the tent. But you could see there were lights on in there. I thought maybe there was a fashion show, or a special episode of *The Apprentice* being filmed there, or something.

Except that the limo pulled over right next to the stairs that head down to the rink. And Michael got out of the car, then held the door open for me to follow.

"Michael," I said. "*What* is going on?"

"Come and see," he said, still grinning.

And he took my hand and led me out of the limo and down the steps to the rink, and the entrance to the big white tent . . .

. . . where a member of the Royal Genovian Secret Service bowed and lifted the flap for us to enter—

—into a winter wonderland! Seriously! Even though it was the first of May, the ice across the rink was hard and smooth! The air inside the tent was chilly—it was being cooled down by about a hundred portable air conditioners! There were snowmakers in every corner sending flurries of white snowflakes into the air . . . snowflakes that were glistening in the hair of this huge group of people standing out on the ice, who all shouted, at the same time, "Happy Sweet Sixteen, Mia!"

I couldn't believe it! A surprise birthday ice-skating party! There was my mom, and Mr. G, and Rocky, and Lilly, and J. P., and Tina, and Boris, and Shameeka, and the guy Shameeka has been dating this year, and Ling Su, and Perin, and the Drs. Moscovitz, and my neighbor Ronnie, and even, of all people, my *DAD*!!!

I never suspected that they were planning something . . . something other than Grandmère's horrible *My Super Royal Sweet Sixteen* thing.

And I certainly never would have expected an *ice-skating* party on my birthday, seeing as how it's just slightly too warm out for skating!

But trust Michael to find a way to give me EXACTLY what I wanted.

Well, pretty much, anyway.

After I'd screamed at everyone for keeping such a big secret from me, I found out that none of them had actually known about it, except for Michael, who'd come up with the idea and arranged the whole thing, and my mom and Mr. G, who'd been in charge of making sure I was in the dark about it. And my dad, who'd paid for it . . . as well as for twenty stationary bikes, which he was donating in my name to AEHS, so we could have spin classes instead of volleyball from time to time. . . .

It's not enough to create a personal workout and health program targeted to every student's own specific health needs. But it was a definite start!

Principal Gupta is going to *die* when they're delivered on Monday.

Everyone had a good laugh over my indignation at Grandmère's plan. "Like I was ever going to let her do any such thing," was what my dad had to say about it (he said he'd tried to invite Grandmère to the skating party, but that she'd declined the invitation. I didn't tell him that was because she's busy taking Andy Milonakis to Genovia. I figured he'll find that out on his own, soon enough).

Even Lilly was like, "You didn't REALLY think I was in on her scheme to put you on MTV, did you?"

Um, yeah. I really did. But I didn't tell her that. Finding out that she really hadn't been was a totally awesome birthday present—but one that made me feel totally terrible when, while we were all chowing down on cake and lacing up our skates, Lilly came over to me and whispered, looking super weird, "I did it. I told him."

At first I didn't think I'd heard her right, because they had the sound system turned up so loud, with Rihanna's "Pon De Replay" blaring. Then I noticed her expression, which was a mixture of dismay and total embarrassment. And I realized what she'd said.

My God. She'd drunk the fat. LILLY DRANK THE FAT!!!!

Even Ross didn't drink the fat when Rachel asked him to. He was GOING to, but at the last minute, she stopped him. . . .

Only I hadn't gotten a chance to stop Lilly from drinking the fat. Because I had never in a million years thought she'd go ahead and do it. I mean, we're best friends, and all.

But that she'd actually gone ahead and DRUNK THE FAT??? I couldn't believe it.

"You TOLD him?" I practically shrieked.

"Shhhh!" Lilly pinched me. A birthday pinch to grow an inch, I guess. "Not so loud! Yes, I told him. That's what you wanted, wasn't it? That's what you said I had to do so you could trust me again. So I did it."

And then I felt the mean little elf that had sprung alive inside me the day before die a quick, ignominious death. What had I been thinking? Why had I asked Lilly to do something so stupid—and humiliating? Telling J. P. she loved him wasn't going to keep her from cheating on him with some other random guy, as she'd done to Boris, or keep her from mortifying me at this, or any other future event. I can't believe I'd asked her to do something so stupid . . . so practically guaranteed to make him run from her like a startled fawn.

But even more, I couldn't believe she'd actually done it.

Glancing over to where J. P.—who was turning out not to be the world's best skater—was being coaxed by Lars to let go of the rink wall, I asked, "What did he say? When you told him, I mean?"

"Thank you," Lilly said softly.

"You're welcome," I said. "I knew if you were just honest with him about your feelings, it would all work out." I'd actually known no such thing, but it seemed like the right thing to say. "But what did he say?"

"That's just it," Lilly said, still not looking very happy. "He said Thank you."

I blinked at her. "Wait . . . you told J. P. you love him, and all he said back was *Thank you*?"

Lilly nodded. She still looked . . . funny. Like she didn't know whether to laugh or cry.

And honestly, I didn't know which she should do either.

"Not exactly an explosion of passion, huh?" Lilly said.

"Not exactly," I said. What could J. P. be thinking? Who says *Thank you* to someone who says they love you? Especially to someone whose tongue has been in your mouth?

Then, because the whole thing was my fault, really, I said, "But it could be, you know, that he didn't know how to reply. I mean, on account of him not being used to having a girlfriend. Or any sort of human interaction, aside from his parents."

Lilly brightened a little. "You think?"

"Totally," I said. And, since Michael had skated up to us at that very moment, I went, "Hey, Michael. If a girl tells a guy that she loves him, and the guy says Thank you, that means he's just not used to that level of intimacy, doesn't it?"

"Sure," Michael says. "Or that he's not that into her. You got a second?"

"J. P. is TOTALLY into you," I assured Lilly, who looked like she was about to kill Michael. "Seriously. Stay here, I'll be right back—"

Then, skating away with Michael, I said, "Why'd you have to say that? She just told J. P. she loves him, and all he said was Thank you!"

"Huh," Michael said, pulling me to the far side of the rink. "Bummer for her. Open your present now."

"My present?" All thoughts of Lilly and her romantic travails left me. "Michael, I thought this party was my present! It's so fantastic . . . the snow, the skating, you and me . . . how did you know this was exactly what I wanted?"

"Because I know you," Michael said, leading me off the ice until we stood in front of a huge box I hadn't noticed before. And I do mean huge. It was taller than me, practically. "Open it."

I opened the enormous cardboard box, and found, standing inside it—

"A Segway Human Transporter!" I shrieked.

"Uh," Michael said quickly. "Not really. I mean, it's a human transporter, but not a Segway. We promised to make each other gifts from now on, remember? So I made you a self-balancing scooter— it's just like a Segway, with the same safety features, redundancy and foolproofing, but it's not the actual—"

"Oh, Michael!" I cried, throwing my arms around his neck. I seriously felt like crying, I was so happy.

Especially when "(I've Had) The Time of My Life," from the *Dirty Dancing* soundtrack, came on over the sound system, and I looked out across the rink and saw my mom skating with Mr. G . . . and Tina skating with Boris . . . and Lars skating with

Janine (don't ask me where she'd come from) . . .
and Shameeka skating with What's-His-Name . . .
and Perin skating with Ling Su (I'll think about that
one later) . . . and Dr. Moscovitz skating with Dr.
Moscovitz, even though they were arguing over the
collective unconscious . . . and even my dad skating
with Ronnie (I'm sure Ronnie will tell him she used
to be a man, sometime). . . .

But, best of all, J. P. skating with Lilly, and not
running from her like a startled fawn, in spite of her
having told him that she loved him.

"Come on, Michael," I said, pulling him back out
onto the ice. "Let's have the time of *our* lives."

And so we did.